YUM, YUM!
by Mara Bergman and Nick Maland

For the wonderful Anne McNeil and thanks to the children and staff of Warren Wood School and Nevill Road Infants, Stockport (MB)
For Mara, Jonathan, and their little dog Noah. With love (NM)

First published in 2009 by Hodder Children's Books

Hodder Children's Books
338 Euston Road, London, NW1 3BH

Hodder Children's Books Australia
Level 17/207 Kent Street, Sydney, NSW 2000

A catalogue record of this book is available from the British Library.

ISBN: 978 0 340 93056 4
10 9 8 7 6 5 4 3 2 1

Printed in China

Hodder Children's Books is a division of Hachette Children's Books
An Hachette Livre UK Company
www.hachettelivre.co.uk

YUM, YUM!

Written by Mara Bergman ✳ Illustrated by Nick Maland

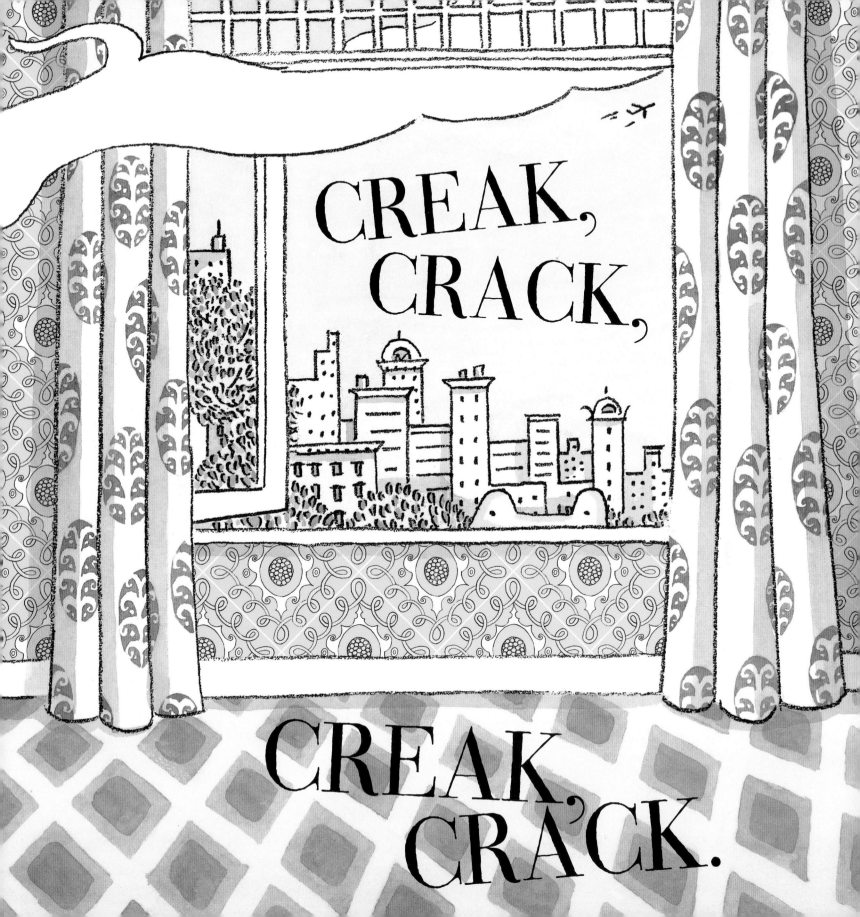

Did anyone see who crept through the window,
long and lean and scaly and green?

Not Katie or James or
their little dog Harry.

CLUMP,
STUMP,

CLUMP, STUMP.

Did anyone see
   who slumped through the window
   with wobbly lips
      and wiggly hips
         and a lumpetty bump
            of a hump?

Not Katie or James
or their little dog Harry.

Hisssssssssssssss, swisssssssssssshhhhh, hissssssssss, swisssssssshhh.

Did anyone see
    who slid through the window,
        slippery as soap
            and skinny as rope?

Not Katie or James or
their little dog Harry.

TRIT,
TROT.

TRIT, TROT.

Did anyone see
who tripped through the window,
neighing and braying
and searching for hay?

Not Katie or James or
their little dog Harry.

EVERYONE saw
who stormed through the window,
rough and ready,
big and heavy,
hairy and just
a little bit scary –
even Katie and James
and their little dog Harry!

SNAP!

HUMPH!

SSSSSSSSSSSSSSSSSSSSSSSSSS!

NEIGH!

EEEEEEEEEEK!

'It's a bear!' someone squeaked.

What was it after?
Something to eat?
A crocodile? A camel?
A snake or a horse?

*KATIE AND JAMES
AND THEIR LITTLE
DOG HARRY,
OF COURSE!*

But the bear wanted bread,
at least that's what he said.
'YUM, YUM!'

Then they ALL wanted some –
with butter and marmalade, honey and jam,
with eggs and cheese, bananas and ham…

But did they EVER go home?
Yes, they certainly did.

The camel left first, then the horse, croc and snake.
The big bear went last, he was searching for…

CAKE!

And when they were gone
a great relief it was too
for Katie and James
and their little dog Harry.

PHEW!